THE WILD BABY

by BARBRO LINDGREN

pictures by EVA ERIKSSON

adapted from the Swedish by JACK PRELUTSKY

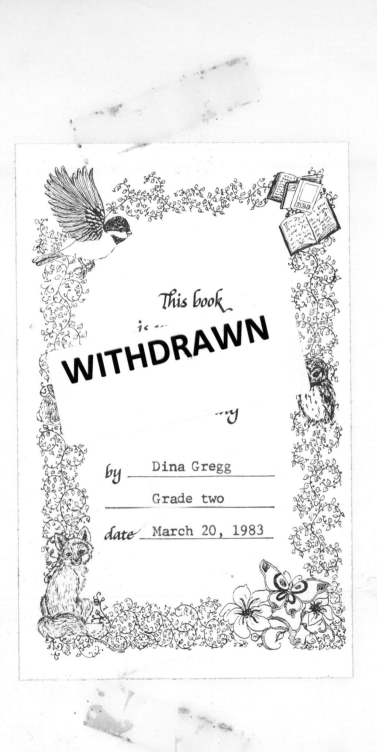

This book

is

WITHDRAWN

by ___Dina Gregg___

___Grade two___

date ___March 20, 1983___

The Wild Baby

⚏ Greenwillow Books, New York

Swedish text copyright © 1980
by Barbro Lindgren
Illustrations copyright © 1980
by Eva Eriksson
English text copyright © 1981
by Jack Prelutsky

Swedish edition entitled
Mamman och den vilda Bebin
published by Raben & Sjögren

10 9 8 7 6 5 4 3 2 1

Library of Congress
Cataloging in Publication Data
Lindgren, Barbro. The wild baby.
Translation of:
Mamman och den vilda bebin.
Summary: Baby Ben gets into
one difficulty after another,
from which Mama rescues him–
but not for long.
[1. Mothers and sons–Fiction.
2. Stories in rhyme]
I. Eriksson, Eva.   II. Title.
PZ8.3.L616 Wi   [E]   81-2151
ISBN 0-688-00600-0   AACR2
ISBN 0-688-00601-9 (lib. bdg.)

Mama loved her baby Ben,
her small and precious child,
but he always disobeyed her,
he was reckless, loud and wild.

He disappeared one morning
when he should have been in bed.

She found him sleeping soundly
in the wooden clock instead.

He crept into her room one night,
she snored and didn't hear,
and softly as the slyest cat
he climbed the chandelier.
He dangled there until it broke,
then hurried out as mama woke.

He fell into the toilet bowl
and so he had to shout,
"Mama! Hurry! Help! I'm stuck!
Please mama! Get me out!"
Mama rushed in, terrified,
and quickly pulled him back outside.

He clambered up the kitchen sink
and dove in for a swim.
He broke a lot of dishes,
mama really scolded him.
"How come you never let me play!"
he grumbled as he stormed away.

He crawled into a big blue sack
and left without a sound,
poor mama hunted vainly,
baby Ben could not be found.

But late that night, the big blue sack
marched right into the hall.
"Hello!" said baby Ben, "I'm back!"
She hugged him, sack and all.

She took him out to get some air,
but all at once he wasn't there.
She shuddered as a car sped by,
and surely was about to cry.

But then she spied him in a tree,
relaxing on a limb,
she sat below, so when he fell,
she softly cushioned him.

Soon afterward, at lunchtime,
baby Ben grew very ill.

He had spots and dots all over,
with a fever and a chill.

So mama put her Ben to bed,
she held his hand, she stroked his head,
she kissed his nose, she rubbed his ears,
he soon was well, she dried her tears.

What happy noises then they made,
as all that night they danced and played.

One day she took him for a stroll,
they walked and walked for hours,
and when they reached a grassy knoll,
she stooped to gather flowers.
But as she picked a small bouquet,
he tiptoed off and slipped away.

When mama saw he wasn't there,
the tears streamed down her face,
she wept and wept in great despair.
"He's gone without a trace.
I'll never find him in the wood,
my baby Ben is lost for good."

Then suddenly, out popped his head,
"A wolf just licked my face," he said.

"I licked him back, he ran away,
we won't *see* *him* again today."
Mama broke into a smile
and hugged him tightly for a while.
She bundled home her baby Ben....

Of course, he's since run off again.